Hugs

JULY 2004.

TO. Jonah.

LOVE nana

Hugs

A special bedtime prayer

Pennie Kidd

Illustrations by
Susie Poole

LION
Children's Books

Hugs in the morning
When the sun begins to shine,

Hugs in the evening
when it's nearly supper time,

Hugs in the daytime
When we go out for a walk,

Hugs in the night-time
When I always want to talk!

Hugs when it's time to go
And I turn to wave goodbye,

Hugs when I hurt myself
And rub my eyes and cry.

Hugs when it's playtime
And my friends make me laugh,

Hugs when it's bedtime
And time to have my bath.

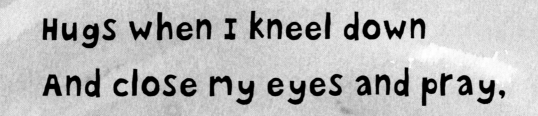

Hugs when I kneel down
And close my eyes and pray,

Hugs when I kiss goodnight
Then talk to God and say...

Thank you God for everyone
That I meet through the day.

Thank you for the smiles and hugs
And love that come my way.

Thank you that I know I'm loved
Especially by you.

Help me always give a hug
And show that I love too.

Published by
Lion Publishing plc
Mayfield House, 256 Banbury Road,
Oxford OX2 7DH, England
www.lion-publishing.co.uk
ISBN 0 7459 4594 5

First hardback edition 2001
First paperback edition 2002
1 3 5 7 9 10 8 6 4 2 0

A catalogue record for this book is available
from the British Library

Typeset in 26/42 Bokka-Solid
Printed and bound in Malaysia